BREAD SONG

by Frederick Lipp

Illustrations by Jason Gaillard

MONDO

for Fred, Hope, Hilary, Bennett, and those whom they cherish.
Thanks to Alison and Matt who invited me to hear the bread sing. –F.L.

for Nelson Fuertes–J.G.

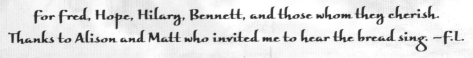

For information contact:
MONDO Publishing, 980 Avenue of the Americas, New York, NY 10018.
Visit our web site at http://www.mondopub.com

Printed in China

04 05 06 07 08 09 10 HC 9 8 7 6 5 4 3 2 1
04 05 06 07 08 09 10 PB 9 8 7 6 5 4 3 2 1
ISBN 1-59336-000-2 (hardcover)   ISBN 1-59336-001-0 (pbk.)
Designed by Martha Rago
Edited by Don L. Curry

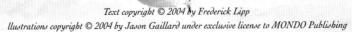

Library of Congress Cataloging-in-Publication Data: Lipp, Frederick. Bread song / Frederick Lipp ;
illustrations Jason Gaillard. p. cm.Summary: Hoping to make Chamnan, an eight-year-old immigrant from Thailand,
feel more at home, the owner of a Portland, Maine, baker invites him and his grandfather to hear her bread sing.
ISBN 1-59336-000-2 – ISBN 1-59336-001-0 (pbk. : alk. paper)
[1. Immigrants--Fiction. 2. Bashfulness--Fiction. 3. Friendship--Fiction. 4. Thai Americans--Fiction.
5. Bread--Fiction. 6. Grandfathers--Fiction. 7. Portland (Me.)--Fiction.] I. Gaillard, Jason, ill. II. Title.
PZ7.L6645Br 2004 [E]--dc21
2003046475

In this old seaport, down a zigzag street, there are two little shops. One sells bread. The other sells food the way it is cooked in Thailand.

The two shops are across the street from one another on Wharf Street. Everyone who works in Alison's Bakery speaks English. Across the street, everyone who works in the restaurant speaks Thai.

One chilly morning not too long ago, a boy and his grandfather talked as they made their way across Wharf Street in a most peculiar manner....

"One, two, three, four steps," Grandfather counted.

"One, two, three, four steps," Chamnan repeated.

Grandfather and Chamnan held hands as they crossed the street counting the cobblestones. Chamnan made sure he stepped on every stone.

Grandfather was teaching Chamnan how to count in English. This counting game was difficult for Chamnan, who was eight years old and living in a new country. The first step began outside the restaurant that Chamnan's father and mother called the Thai Mountain Restaurant.

"Five, six, seven, eight steps," Grandfather continued in his strong voice.

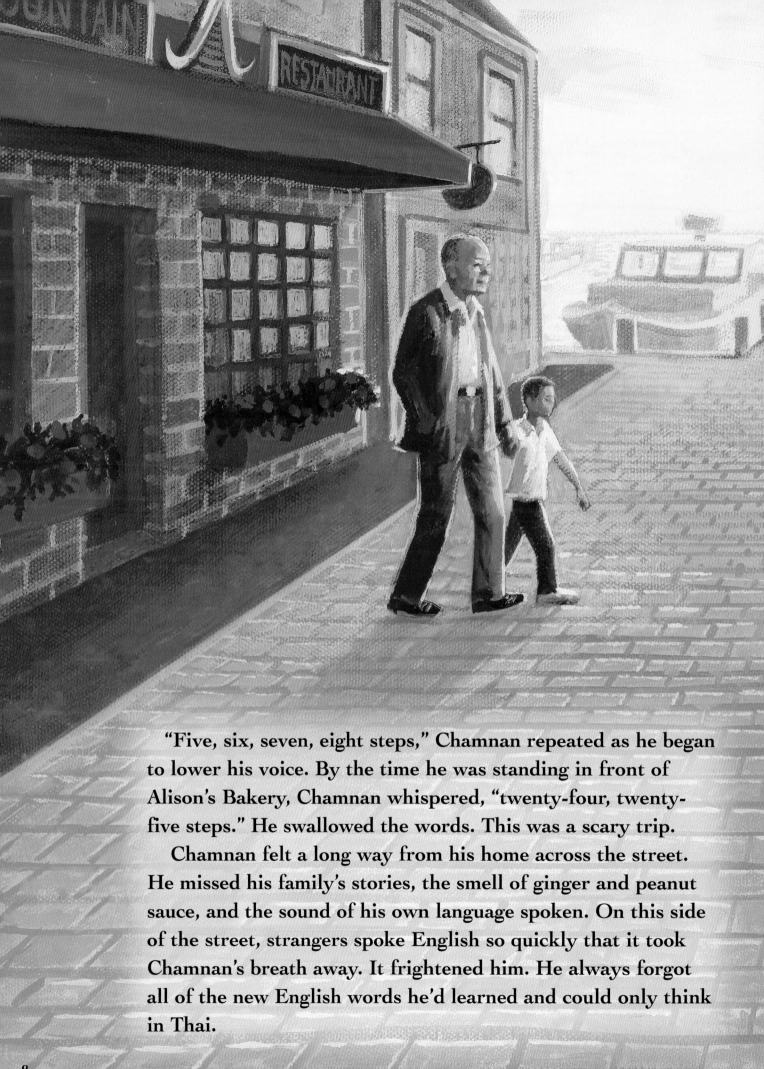

"Five, six, seven, eight steps," Chamnan repeated as he began to lower his voice. By the time he was standing in front of Alison's Bakery, Chamnan whispered, "twenty-four, twenty-five steps." He swallowed the words. This was a scary trip.

Chamnan felt a long way from his home across the street. He missed his family's stories, the smell of ginger and peanut sauce, and the sound of his own language spoken. On this side of the street, strangers spoke English so quickly that it took Chamnan's breath away. It frightened him. He always forgot all of the new English words he'd learned and could only think in Thai.

Before they even reached Alison's Bakery,
the smell of flour and yeast slipped through the
cracks around the door and greeted them in the street.
Chamnan breathed deeply. The salt air of the nearby sea
mixed with the smell of freshly baked bread until Chamnan
felt he could fly like a seagull.

"Ah, Chamnan, take a deep breath," Grandfather said.
"Enjoy the fragrance of raisins and cinnamon mixed with the
air of the sea."

Chamnan said nothing. His smile told his grandfather that
he was happy to hold his hand. The air was full of sweet-
smelling goodness . . . spices . . . burnt sugar.

Inside the bakery, people were jammed together, all waiting in line for bread, rolls, and muffins.

After Bill the fisherman paid for his three muffins, he turned to Chamnan. "Hi, Chamnan, what are you going to buy from the baker today?"

Chamnan, too shy to speak, shrugged his shoulders and smiled. Bill tousled Chamnan's hair as he winked and walked away.

In the little cubbyhole of a store, Chamnan waited as people laughed and talked about the weather, football, and the news. Chamnan was getting hungrier by the minute. His stomach was beginning to growl and make all kinds of noises that he was sure everyone in the bakery could hear.

ALISON'S
BAKERY

Finally, it was Chamnan's and his grandfather's turn.

Grandfather said, "Please, I'll have one baguette." The baguette was a long, skinny loaf of bread. It looked like a log, Chamnan thought. And where the crust curled back, it seemed like the bark of a tree.

"What will you have this morning, Chamnan?" Grandfather asked.

Chamnan pinched his fingers together, making a sign for little.

"Little bread?" Grandfather asked.

Chamnan nodded yes and pointed to a glass jar next to the cash register.

"That's called chocolate biscotti. Can you say that?"

Chamnan smiled and looked at the floor.

"Don't worry, Chamnan. You may have your little bread," Grandfather said comfortingly.

Alison, the baker, was always kind and happy. She reached into the jar and placed the little bread in Chamnan's hand. As soon as he returned home, Chamnan unwrapped the tissue paper and dipped the little chocolate bread into a glass of cold milk. Then, popping it into his mouth, he smacked his lips and looked out the window at the fishing boats in the harbor.

Later that afternoon, as Alison mixed flour and water in a large shiny bowl, an idea jumped into her head. She looked across the street and suddenly knew a secret that might help Chamnan get over his shyness.

After work, Alison walked across the street and into the
Thai Mountain Restaurant. She noticed Chamnan peeking at
her from behind a large flowering tree.

"Hello, Chamnan, will you please come and help me order
something good to eat?"

Chamnan was so proud of his family's restaurant and so glad to see Alison that he quickly moved to stand beside her chair. He was too shy to speak English, but his smile was brave.

After looking at the menu, Chamnan pointed to a picture of spring rolls. He nodded his head up and down to indicate that this would be a good choice. Soon Grandfather came and greeted Alison.

Grandfather told Alison about the beautiful green mountains around their home in Thailand. He told stories about the gentle ways of the people.

Alison listened carefully, hoping that one day she might visit the place where Chamnan was born . . . but for now she was planning an adventure across the street.

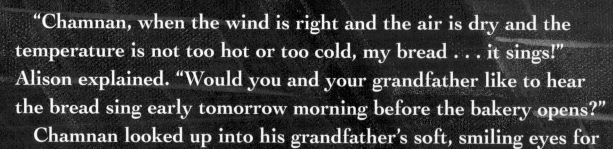

"Chamnan, when the wind is right and the air is dry and the temperature is not too hot or too cold, my bread . . . it sings!" Alison explained. "Would you and your grandfather like to hear the bread sing early tomorrow morning before the bakery opens?"

Chamnan looked up into his grandfather's soft, smiling eyes for an answer.

"Ah, yes," Grandfather said. "We could come tomorrow morning. I wonder, how does bread sing?"

That night, Chamnan snuggled into his bed over the restaurant, listening to the clinking of dishes and glasses, and to the chatter of people. As he fell asleep, he began dreaming about the mystery of bread singing.

In the early morning darkness, Chamnan took his grandfather's hand. Together they quickly walked the twenty-five steps over the bumpy cobblestones of the zigzag street. They were so excited about their adventure, they forgot to count the steps.

Alison greeted them before they knocked on the door.

"Come in! You are just in time to hear the music bread makes when it comes hot out of the oven," Alison said as she gently guided Chamnan and his grandfather into the center of the room. They could see the long ovens with row after row of Grandfather's favorite bread.

The timer bell rang, telling Alison the bread was ready. She took a long flat paddle and scooped up five loaves at a time. She shoveled them onto the cooling racks that towered high above Chamnan's head. There was no time to talk. Chamnan and his grandfather were soon surrounded by hundreds of loaves of bread.

Alison put the paddle down as little beads of perspiration covered her forehead. Her cheeks were red. She was out of breath from the heavy work.

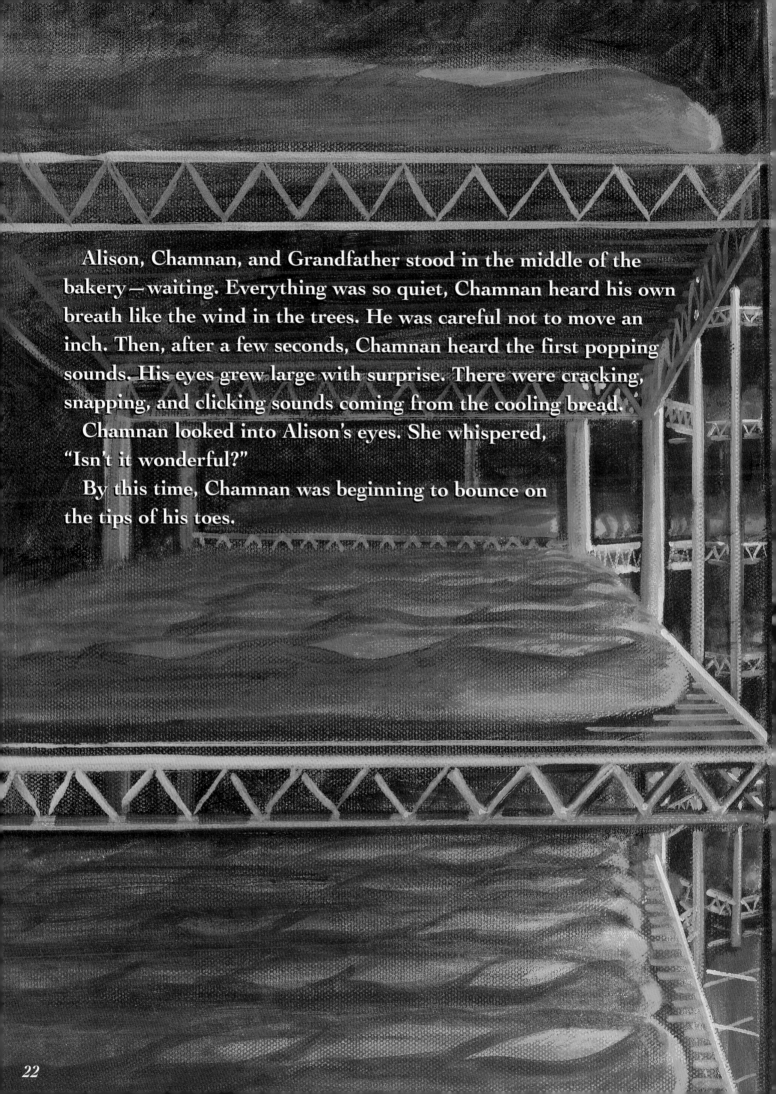

Alison, Chamnan, and Grandfather stood in the middle of the bakery—waiting. Everything was so quiet, Chamnan heard his own breath like the wind in the trees. He was careful not to move an inch. Then, after a few seconds, Chamnan heard the first popping sounds. His eyes grew large with surprise. There were cracking, snapping, and clicking sounds coming from the cooling bread.

Chamnan looked into Alison's eyes. She whispered, "Isn't it wonderful?"

By this time, Chamnan was beginning to bounce on the tips of his toes.

Alison took his hand and drew him closer to the bread. The heat from the loaves felt like bright sunshine on a hot summer's day. He leaned closer.

"Be careful, the bread is very hot," Alison cautioned.

As the bread popped and crackled, little puffs of steam shot from the cracks in the crust. Each fountain of steam whistled sweetly. Chamnan wiggled his fingers, making believe he was playing a flute.

All of a sudden, Chamnan felt at home. His tongue loosened. Words danced in his head.

"What do you hear, Chamnan?" Alison asked.

Hopping on one foot and then the other, Chamnan whistled, snapped his fingers, and tried to say crackle all at the same time. He couldn't stop laughing.

Chamnan took a deep breath and spoke a whole sentence in Thai. "Kanom pung rong pleng." Surprised by the sound of his own voice, he then said in English, "The bread sings!" Grandfather was so happy to hear his grandson speak in English that he cried happy tears.

By this time, all the early customers who had come for their morning rolls and bread were peeking through the window, waiting for Alison to unlock the door. They watched Chamnan listening to the bread. When the door opened, Bill the fisherman was the first in line behind Chamnan.

Alison asked, "Chamnan, what would you like this morning?"

"Ah...please, one...baguette for my grandfather...and one...chocolate biscotti for me," Chamnan said.

Those in line, who had never heard Chamnan speak before, grinned. Alison was so happy she hugged herself, and Bill the fisherman clapped four times.

When everyone was quiet, Chamnan said in Thai,
"Kanom pung rong pleng." Then with a shy smile he said
the same thing in English. "The bread sings!"

No one knew what to say. This day was better than six currant scones, three French rolls, and a dozen sticky buns.

Before leaving the crowd in the bakery, Chamnan waved and said, "Lagon." This was the Thai way of saying good-bye!

"Lagon," the crowd echoed.

Chamnan left the bakery with the sound of the bread song in his ears. After taking his grandfather's hand, Chamnan counted as he marched home, "One, two, three, four, five, six, seven, eight, nine. . . ."

When Chamnan reached twenty-five steps, he turned and looked across the street at Alison's Bakery. It was not so very far away after all.